Contemporary Asian Americans
SEIJI OZAWA

BY
SHERI TAN

RAINTREE
STECK-VAUGHN
P U B L I S H E R S
The Steck-Vaughn Company

Austin, Texas

Copyright © 1997, Steck-Vaughn Company. All rights reserved. No part of this book may be reproduced or utilized in any form or by any means, electronic or mechanical, including photocopying, recording, or by any information storage and retrieval system, without permission in writing from the copyright owner. Requests for permission to make copies of any part of the work should be mailed to: Copyright Permissions, Steck-Vaughn Company, P.O. Box 26015, Austin, Texas 78755.

Published by Raintree Steck-Vaughn, an imprint of Steck-Vaughn Company.
Produced by Mega-Books, Inc.
Design and Art Direction by Michaelis/Carpelis Design Associates.
Cover photo: ©Antonio Ribeiro/Gamma-Liaison

Library of Congress Cataloging-in-Publication Data
Tan, Sheri.
　　Seiji Ozawa / Sheri Tan.
　　　　p.　　cm — (Contemporary Asian Americans)
　　Includes bibliographical references (p. 47) and index.
　　Summary: A biography of the famous Japanese conductor, a citizen of both Japan and the United States, who has achieved international recognition for his skills in interpreting western music.
　　ISBN 0-8172-3993-6 (Hardcover)
　　ISBN 0-8172-6882-0 (Softcover)
　　1. Ozawa, Seiji, 1935- — Juvenile literature.　2. Conductors (Music) — Biography — Juvenile literature.　[1. Ozawa, Seiji, 1935-.　2. Conductors (Music)　3. Japanese Americans — Biography.]　I. Title.　II. Series.
ML3930.095T36　1997
784.2'092 — dc21　　　　　　　　　　　　　　　　　　　　　　96-48640
[B]　　　　　　　　　　　　　　　　　　　　　　　　　　　　　　　CIP
　　　　　　　　　　　　　　　　　　　　　　　　　　　　　　AC　MN
Printed and bound in the United States.

1 2 3 4 5 6 7 8 9 LB 00 99 98 97 96

Photo credits: ©Victoria Brynner/Gamma Liaison: pp.4, 44; AP/Wide World Photos, Inc.: pp. 7, 28, 31, 36; ©Lincoln Russell/Boston Symphony Orchestra: p. 9; ©Steve Hansen/Time Magazine: p. 10, UPI/Corbis-Bettmann: pp. 12, 14; Corbis-Bettmann: p. 17; ©Costa Manos/Magnum Photos, Inc.: pp. 18, 35; ©Stu Rosner/Boston Symphony Orchestra: p. 21; ©William Mercer/Boston Symphony Orchestra: p. 22; ©Whitestone Photo/Heinz H. Weissenstein/Boston Symphony Orchestra: p. 24; ©Suzanne Estel/San Francisco Performing Arts Library & Museum: p. 27; ©Rick Friedman/Black Star: p. 32; ©1994 Steve Rosenthal/William Rawn Assoc., Architects, Inc./Boston Symphony Orchestra: p. 39; ©Michael Lutch/Boston Symphony Orchestra: p. 41; ©Ira Wyman/Boston Symphony Orchestra: p. 43.

Contents

1 An International Star Is Born 5

2 From Tokyo to Paris 11

3 A Dream Comes True 20

4 Culture Clash 26

5 At Home with the Boston Symphony 30

6 Opening Doors and Building Bridges 40

Important Dates 46

Glossary 47

Bibliography 47

Index 48

Chapter *One*

AN INTERNATIONAL STAR IS BORN

The hall was silent as the young conductor on the stage raised his baton. The music began. The conductor, a 24-year-old musician, stood in front of the **orchestra** and seemed to put his whole body into his work. The players responded wholeheartedly to his enthusiasm and energy. When the music's final note was played, Seiji Ozawa became not only one of the youngest musicians, but also the first Japanese to win the top prize at the famous International Competition of Orchestra Conductors, in Besançon (beh-ZAHN-sohn), France. From that day on, Seiji would impress many more musicians and audiences and make his mark in the world of Western music.

This competition took place in 1959. Few Asian

Seiji Ozawa was the first Asian conductor to receive international recognition in the world of Western classical music.

musicians at that time performed Western music in concert. Even fewer were recognized internationally for their work. It was not easy for the young Seiji Ozawa, with his dark hair and Asian face, to stand in front of a row of 24 European judges and try to convince them that he understood Western classical music, let alone conduct an entire orchestra. To them he was an outsider. Seiji felt a strong need to prove that he had a place in "their" world.

European music was first brought to Japan by Portuguese and Spanish **missionaries** in the 16th century. However, the Japanese government decided that Western thinking and ways of life were not a good influence on the Japanese people. It was not until the latter part of the 19th century that European music was heard once again in Japan. During this time the government was eager to establish good relations with Europe and the United States. Most of the music that came to Japan then was in the form of military band music and Christian hymns. The government even encouraged Western music to be taught in Japanese schools.

Many foreign musicians and music teachers, especially from Germany and Russia, were invited to perform and teach in Japan. Later on, in the early 20th century, a few Japanese musicians were encouraged to further their musical studies in Europe. This number would probably have grown at a faster rate if wars, political differences, and prejudices had not gotten in

Ever since Seiji paved the way, many Asian musicians have achieved success in the West, including the young violinist Midori (left).

the way. But because of these factors, the number of Asians in the world of Western music remained small. Certainly none of them received the worldwide recognition that such musicians as the cellist Yo-Yo Ma and the violinists Midori and Kyung Wha-Chung do today.

It was this acceptance and recognition that Seiji Ozawa was looking for the day he stood in front of the judges at the Besancon competition in 1959. He knew the task he had set for himself was not an easy one. He had only recently arrived in Europe, eager to learn all he could about conducting and to fulfill his dream of becoming a professional conductor. He spoke very little English. He realized that there were people who would judge how well he understood Western music and how well he could conduct based on what he looked like and how well he spoke. Seiji knew that this was not fair. But he believed that the best way to change people's minds was to demonstrate his talent and simply do his best. He may not have been able to communicate through words, but there was another language he was familiar with—one he knew the judges could understand. This was a language that could not only bridge the communication gap but also make people pay attention to him. It was the language of music.

"My one rule is to avoid words," Seiji once said. "As soon as you speak, you limit yourself. There are only three or four words for happiness. But music has maybe two dozen ways to express it. I try to speak with my body, my face, my baton."

Think of how circus clowns are able to make people laugh, feel sad, or feel happy and excited. These performers do not use their voices to speak, but by using their whole bodies—including arms, hands, legs, faces, mouths, and eyes—they can make people understand what they are trying to say.

This is also what Seiji does well. He uses his body to conduct a piece of music so that the musicians know the exact emotion that he wants them to convey. When the musicians can translate the conductor's actions into beautiful music, the audience can enjoy

Seiji uses music to convey the emotions and moods that classical composers wanted listeners to feel.

the music as it is meant to be played and feel happy, sad, or excited, too.

There were many talented musicians from all over the world at the famous competition in Besançon. Seiji did his best. This was his big chance to show everyone that he had the ability and the passion to conduct Western classical music, no matter what he looked like or what country he was from. If Seiji did not win the competition, he felt that he would not be able to pursue his dream. Seiji knew that his teacher and his family believed in him. His confidence was

Conducting a symphony orchestra is the fulfillment of a lifetime dream for Seiji.

high, because he had made it this far—he knew there was no turning back.

There are few words to express what Seiji felt when the results of the competition were finally announced and he learned that he had won. He had traveled thousands of miles to prove to the world that he could be a professional conductor. Now he had been given the chance. Seiji Ozawa's new life was about to begin. After so many years of hard work, he had taken his first step toward becoming a professional conductor.

Chapter

FROM TOKYO TO PARIS

Seiji Ozawa was born on September 1, 1935, in Shenyang, China. His parents were Japanese, living in a part of China that was then called Manchuria. At the time Manchuria had been taken over by the Japanese. Seiji's father was a dentist for the railroad company there. He was also a pacifist (someone who doesn't believe that war can solve problems). The Japanese were heavily involved in World War II, but Seiji's father stood firmly by his beliefs. The Japanese government did not like that Seiji's father disagreed with them. They decided to **deport** Seiji, his three brothers, and his parents back to Japan in 1944. Seiji was just nine years old.

When they returned to Japan, Seiji and his family lived in Tachikawa, just outside of Tokyo. Life was not any easier for the Ozawa family once they were back in their homeland. Because of his belief that war was a terrible thing, Seiji's father was not allowed to make a living as a dentist. He became a rice farmer but made very little money, and the family remained poor.

It was a very hard time for Seiji and his brothers. It was also a scary time because they lived near a military air base. The base was the target of attacks from American and European armed forces. The young boys often saw bombs being dropped from planes.

"I went to elementary school every day," Seiji recalled to a reporter. "But when a bomber came, and the siren sounded, everybody had to go underground. Every house had a bomb shelter. The school didn't have one. Everyone had to go home."

Times were difficult for the Ozawa family when they lived near Tokyo, Japan, during World War II. Seiji's father worked as a rice farmer to make ends meet.

The sirens warned everyone that a plane was near and bombs were about to be dropped. While the war dragged on, bombs and sirens were as common as the sound of fire trucks. Imagine having to run every time you heard a fire truck coming down the street! You might even be afraid that the next bomb was going to hit your house. That's what it was like for Seiji.

"It becomes like part of life, a bomber coming over every few days," Seiji said. "When that happens, you don't want to leave school and go home. You're swimming, and the other boys say, 'Nah, don't bother.' My young brother and I sometimes did not get out when the bombing started. It was very dangerous."

And a very sad thing did happen. A bomb destroyed the homes of three of Seiji's friends from school. The young boys were killed instantly.

One day Seiji was standing outside his home when he saw a bomber flying toward the air base. He remembers this moment well because it was the first time he saw a non-Asian face.

"He was coming at me, shooting at something. But really he was 20 meters [65 feet] away. Bullets made the sand blow up in front of me. I had no time to go inside. It came so close. I could see his eyes. It was a very strange experience."

The war continued to be a sad time for Seiji and his family. His uncle, his father's youngest brother, was a military doctor stationed in the city of Hiroshima. The American government felt that the only way to stop

Seiji attended an elementary school much like the one pictured here, which just barely survived a bombing. The constant threat of bombings was a fact of life during Seiji's early years.

the war was to attack Japan. Hiroshima was the city chosen to be the target for the world's first atomic bomb. When the bomb hit the city, 80,000 people were killed. Many of them died instantly. Seiji's uncle was not in the city when the bomb was dropped, but because he was a doctor, he immediately rushed back to help take care of the injured. Like many people in the city, he was exposed to the harmful **radiation** that remained after the bombing. Seiji's uncle became sick and later died of cancer caused by the radiation.

After the bombing in Hiroshima, a second atomic bomb was dropped on Nagasaki. As a result of the destruction, the war ended. The Japanese decided to surrender because they did not want to suffer any more bombings. By this time it was August 1945.

Seiji's father could not have been happier. He was looking forward to the new freedom that the Japanese people would enjoy. "Now we can have happy things like baseball and music instead of war!" Seiji recalled his father saying.

During the war all music had been under the strict control of the government. The Japanese people were not encouraged to listen to European and American music. However, Seiji's parents had allowed Seiji and his brothers to listen to this music and to play along using Western musical instruments. Seiji had first heard Western music when he went with his mother to church services in China. During this time, when the family was in China, Seiji began to take piano lessons. He enjoyed playing pieces by composers such as Beethoven, Brahms, Bach, and Mendelssohn.

One time during the war, Seiji's father heard that a piano was being sold for a small sum of money. The only problem with buying the piano was that the instrument was in Yokohama, a city about 25 miles away from where they lived. Seiji's father had just enough money to pay for the piano but not enough to pay someone to bring the piano to their home. So he and one of Seiji's brothers took a cart, traveled to Yokohama by foot, and brought the piano back to their farm. It took them two whole days of traveling!

Clearly Seiji's father really loved Western music. You can see why he was so happy when the war was over. Everyone could once again enjoy Western music without feeling guilty or being secretive.

Japanese music, like Western music, uses string instruments, wind instruments, and drums. However, Japanese instruments are quite different from Western instruments. They produce sounds that are not like those in Western music. Some of the instruments are: *koto*, a long string instrument that is like the Western **zither**; *shamisen*, another string instrument that is similar to the Western **lute**; and *shakuhachi*, which is a flutelike instrument. *Taiko* drums are huge instruments set on stands that require the drummers to use long sticks and to beat the drums with the force of their whole bodies. The drummers work up a sweat as they jump high and use all their strength to beat the drums. It is quite exciting to watch!

Traditionally in Japanese culture, music is usually combined with dance and drama to form a kind of play, called *noh*. People who are not familiar with Japanese music may find the different tones, rhythms, and pitches used in Japanese music somewhat strange.

Another interesting difference between traditional Japanese music and Western music is that most Japanese music is played from memory. There are no music scores. Musicians are required to concentrate by carefully listening to and watching their teachers. It is only under the recent influence of Western music, where

The *shamisen* is a two-stringed Japanese instrument something like a lute. It is played by plucking or strumming the strings.

detailed notes are made for each instrument, that traditional Japanese musicians have begun to write down the music to their pieces. Even then the scores are not complete. They are written in outline form, and only people who are familiar with the piece can really understand and play the music.

As Seiji grew older, his parents realized that playing Western music was not just a hobby for their son. He wanted to be a professional musician. It was not hard for Seiji to decide that this was what he wanted to do, especially after he had watched the performances of the Boston Symphony Orchestra when they toured Japan. Seiji eagerly looked forward to their concerts. The music director and conductor of the orchestra at the

When Seiji was a young boy in Japan, he attended a concert given by the Boston Symphony Orchestra. Little did he know that one day he would conduct that very same orchestra.

time was Charles Münch, and Seiji greatly admired him.

So when Seiji was 16 years old, he enrolled at the Toho School of Music in Tokyo, one of the best music schools in the country. Students learned how to play musical instruments, compose music, and conduct orchestras.

When Seiji joined the school, his ambition was to be a concert pianist. But then he broke both of his index fingers while playing rugby. Although he was upset, Seiji knew he still wanted to be a professional musician. He decided to study conducting and composing instead. It didn't take long for him to find out that he was good at conducting.

Seiji felt that Western music was a natural fit for him.

18

"Western music is so organized," he said in a later interview. "It is so strong and logical that it is very easy for every nationality to learn."

Seiji had an excellent teacher named Hideo Saito. Hideo Saito saw that the young boy had talent, plus an energetic spirit and determination—qualities that a professional conductor should have. He encouraged Seiji to work hard and develop his creative spirit. Hideo Saito knew that Seiji could go far and become a professional conductor. He also felt that the only way for this to happen was for Seiji to go abroad to further his studies. Seiji's teacher and family decided that the young man should go to France.

In 1959 Seiji graduated from the Toho School, with top prizes in composition and conducting. As a student Seiji had some experience conducting the Japan Philharmonic and the NHK, or Nihon Hoso Kyokai (Japanese Broadcasting Company), Symphony Orchestra. Now the real test was about to begin. He could conduct Western music in Japan, but would Westerners give him the opportunity to conduct Western music in Europe or America? How would they regard him? These were questions he could not yet answer. But the one thing Seiji was sure of was his belief in himself. He knew that he would succeed.

Chapter *Three*

A DREAM COMES TRUE

Two important people who paid special attention to Seiji's performance at the International Competition of Orchestra Conductors in Besançon were Charles Münch and Eugène Bigot. They were both very impressed with Seiji's ability. At that time **Maestro** Münch was conductor of the Boston Symphony Orchestra. He invited Seiji to study at the Berkshire Music Center in Tanglewood, Massachusetts, where the Boston Symphony performed in the summer.

It was a great honor to be asked—especially by the man Seiji had so admired while he was growing up in Japan. Tanglewood is located in the Berkshire Mountains in western Massachusetts, near the town of Lenox. The surroundings are very green and peaceful, giving both the performers and music fans a chance to enjoy nature and beautiful music at the same time.

Before crossing the Atlantic Ocean to study at the Berkshire Music Center, Seiji studied conducting with

Seiji (standing on podium, left) leads the Boston Symphony Orchestra and the Tanglewood Festival Chorus at the Berkshire Music Center in Tanglewood, Massachusetts.

Maestro Bigot in Paris for a few months. While in Paris Seiji sold motor scooters for Honda, the Japanese company, to make money for food and shelter. He traveled all over France and Italy selling these scooters.

Seiji enjoyed being in Tanglewood and continued to work hard during the time he was at the Music Center. A Tanglewood education is seen as a very important step toward becoming a professional musician. More than 20 percent of the members of America's major orchestras graduated from the Berkshire Music Center, among them the famous conductors Zubin Mehta and Leonard Bernstein. Since it was established in 1948, the Music Center has attracted thousands of students, who come from all over the world to study composition, conducting, opera, and instrumental performance. Tanglewood has become a place where aspiring musicians can learn from the top musicians and teachers. Besides going to classes, the students are asked to perform with the center's orchestra, choir, and **chamber music** group. These students also get the chance to take part in the Tanglewood Music Festival, a musical event held every summer.

Concertgoers at the Tanglewood Music Festival enjoy a picnic on the lawn before a concert. Concerts are performed in the covered area in the background, called The Music Shed.

As Seiji learned at Tanglewood and continued to realize over the years, a conductor is not simply a person who stands in front of an orchestra and keeps time to the music. A conductor is someone who inspires the orchestra, challenges his or her fellow musicians to do their best, and guides them to work well with one another to create the music.

Conducting involves being completely familiar with all parts of music-making: what types of sounds each instrument makes, the composition of the musical piece, and what the composer is trying to convey. A good conductor knows many music scores thoroughly and is able to help the musicians understand the meaning of a piece. Seiji had to not only learn many music scores but also be able to "hear" them in his mind. Then he would know what sounded correct or incorrect when the orchestra played them.

At the end of the term, Seiji won the Music Center's highest honor for an outstanding student conductor, the Koussevitzky Prize. This prize was named after Serge Koussevitzky, the Russian conductor who headed the Boston Symphony Orchestra from 1924 to 1949. It was Maestro Koussevitzky who started the Berkshire Music Center.

Maestro Koussevitzky had a famous **protégé** named Leonard Bernstein. Little did Seiji know that he was soon to meet Maestro Bernstein, who in turn would take the young Japanese musician under his wing and make him his protégé.

Seiji Ozawa with composer Lukas Foss (left) and Maestro Leonard Bernstein (center). Seiji was not yet 30 years old when this photograph was taken.

What could make a student conductor's experience more wonderful than Seiji's was now? News soon came that Maestro Herbert von Karajan was offering Seiji an apprenticeship with the Berlin Philharmonic Orchestra. Seiji packed his bags and headed back to Europe. Maestro von Karajan was very influential in the world of German music. He was considered master of the symphony and opera, and he could conduct all scores from memory. That is an amazing feat.

While Seiji was studying in Berlin, he came to the attention of Leonard Bernstein. Like others, Maestro Bernstein was taken with Seiji's energy, enthusiasm, and creativity. So impressed was he with the young man that Maestro Bernstein invited Seiji to come with him on the New York Philharmonic's 1961 tour of Japan and offered him the position of assistant conductor for the 1961–1962 season. What a thrill it was to be working with one of the best conductors in the world. It was a dream come true for a 27-year-old musician!

Chapter

CULTURE CLASH

The year 1962 was full of highs and lows for Seiji Ozawa. In January he conducted his first American orchestra, the San Francisco Symphony Orchestra. His years of hard work had paid off. He felt very proud to be standing in front of both musicians and an audience and to be accepted as a professional. The concert was a success.

Feeling confident about his ability, Seiji was looking forward to sharing all the things that he had learned in the last three years, as well as some new ideas, with Japanese musicians of the famous NHK Symphony Orchestra. He was scheduled to conduct a series of concerts later that year with the orchestra in Japan. Unfortunately, in Japan he would not receive the same acceptance or hear that same applause he had heard in San Francisco.

When Seiji stepped onto the Suntory Hall stage in Tokyo for the first rehearsal, he thought his fellow

Seiji rehearsing the San Francisco Symphony Orchestra. This was the first time an Asian conductor led an American orchestra.

Japanese would be proud of the many things he had accomplished in so short a time. After all, he had received the respect and praise of many Westerners.

But Seiji was sadly mistaken. What the Japanese musicians saw on the stage was a young, arrogant conductor who was only interested in showing off his skills. The musicians were not used to a lot of guidance from their conductors. Most Japanese musicians at that time thought it was their job to simply perform the music. They felt that Seiji was too Westernized. When they watched Seiji conduct, they thought he was criticizing them openly. The orchestra members were sure he was trying to make them sound different from the way they usually played.

"We won't be bullied by that kid," the musicians said. They felt that when Seiji told them exactly what to correct, he was not respecting them. He even had his own interpretation of the music he wanted them to play. Did Seiji think that they were not good enough and that he had to show them how to play?

The orchestra felt Seiji had turned his back on his Japanese heritage and become too Western in his thinking. It did not matter how many prizes he had won or how famous he was becoming in the West. Rather than being proud of him, they were insulted. To them he seemed to be thinking only of himself and not of the group.

It took a while for Asian musicians to accept Seiji's conducting style, which is a blend of East and West. Here he conducts the New Japan Philharmonic.

This is where Japanese and Western cultures clash. Western culture encourages people to be individuals and voice their own ideas. But Japanese culture praises those who work well in a team. This means that everybody must have the same ideas. The Japanese feel this is the way to make sure that efforts are successful.

So the NHK Symphony Orchestra flatly refused to work with him. They did not show up for practices. They left Seiji standing on the concert stage alone. Seiji was to have conducted three concerts with the orchestra, but all of them were canceled.

As he left Japan, Seiji was reminded of the Japanese proverb, "The nail that sticks out must be hammered down." This means that for the Japanese, anyone who stands out and is different from the group must be forced to fit in with the group. It was a hard lesson for Seiji. He realized that he would have to find a balance between his Japanese heritage and his life as a conductor of Western music living in the West.

Chapter

AT HOME WITH THE BOSTON SYMPHONY

When he returned to the United States, Seiji was kept busy with many offers. From 1964 to 1968, he was the music director of the Ravinia Festival in Illinois, which is where the Chicago Symphony Orchestra performs during the summer. He was also the music director of the Toronto Symphony Orchestra. In 1970 he became the music director of the San Francisco Symphony.

Seiji learned a great deal by working with all these different orchestras. Getting to know each orchestra was like making a new friend. Just as you would learn what your new friend likes or dislikes, and what he or she is good at, Seiji not only had to learn the personality of each orchestra, he also had to get to know each member of the orchestra. This is not easy; there are usually about 100 members to meet.

To Seiji, working with new orchestras was exciting. He liked getting to know the musicians and finding out their strengths and weaknesses. By learning all that he could about the members of the orchestras, Seiji could inspire the performers to play their best. He challenged the musicians to improve upon their weaknesses and take advantage of their strengths. In this way Seiji believed they would all create music as it was meant to be played.

As Seiji traveled and lived in different cities, music lovers all over the world who had not seen him conduct before were now able to see and appreciate

During the late 1960s, Seiji conducted the Boston Symphony Orchestra at the Tanglewood Music Festival.

what Charles Münch, Herbert von Karajan, and Leonard Bernstein had seen in him. Seiji's work with various orchestras was something he could not have learned from classroom lessons, and the opportunities he had received as music director of these groups were very important. These experiences allowed him him to grow and develop as a conductor.

In 1970 Seiji was also asked to be artistic director of the Berkshire Music Festival in Tanglewood—the very same place where he had studied so many years before. It was like a homecoming, especially because the Boston Symphony Orchestra had played an important role in his early musical experiences.

Seiji Ozawa was the first Asian to be named music director of the Boston Symphony Orchestra.

A few years later, in 1973, Seiji Ozawa made history by being the first Asian musician to be chosen as music director of the Boston Symphony Orchestra. Seiji had come a long way in his career and had now found an important place in the world of Western music.

The orchestra is one of Boston's major cultural institutions. It was founded in 1881 and has long defined classical music in the United States. Guided by European musicians since its founding, the influences of German (among others, George Henschel, the first conductor of the orchestra), French (Charles Münch), and Russian (Serge Koussevitzky) conductors were strong. The addition of Seiji Ozawa has only served to add to the orchestra's rich musical and cultural background.

Boston, the capital of Massachusetts, is the largest city in New England. It is the home of so many famous cultural institutions that many people have nicknamed it "the Athens of America." Its reputation as a leader in music education began early in the 18th century with the establishment of singing schools. Gradually, with many European musicians making Boston their home and community leaders supporting the development of the arts, more music schools were established. The New England Conservatory, the Boston Conservatory of Music, and the Berklee School of Music are among the best music schools in the country.

When Henry Lee Higginson, a banker, gave one million dollars to establish a resident orchestra in Boston, his purpose was to support a group "which should play the best music in the best way and give concerts to all who could pay a small price."

Today the Boston Symphony Orchestra is made up of about 110 members. Seiji Ozawa has led this orchestra for more than 20 years, making him the longest-serving music director now active in North America. However, making history doesn't seem so unusual for Seiji. He has been doing that ever since he first decided to pursue his dream of becoming a professional conductor.

In his years with the orchestra, Seiji Ozawa has led it on numerous international tours. One tour went to China in 1979. No other American orchestra had ever paid an official cultural visit to China before. This tour was recorded in a television documentary that was shown on the PBS network.

Seiji has also taken the Boston Symphony on five visits to Japan, seven tours to Europe, a world tour celebrating the 100th anniversary of the orchestra in 1981, and a debut tour to South America in 1992. It took courage for Seiji to once again tour Japan, where years before he had left feeling misunderstood and unappreciated. In 1978, when the orchestra visited Japan, there was a different feeling in the air. By then the Japanese musicians realized Seiji was not a show-off but an experienced musician whose only desire was to encourage them to create wonderful music. They were respectful and proud of what he had accomplished. They were especially proud that Seiji is respected and admired all over the world.

When the Boston Symphony Orchestra was on tour in China in 1979, Seiji took time out to work with a young music student.

One concert in Japan that will stand out in Seiji's memory took place in January 1995. He was scheduled to conduct the NHK Symphony Orchestra, the very same orchestra that had refused to play for him more than thirty years before.

As Seiji was preparing for the important concert, an earthquake hit Kobe, a city about 300 miles southwest of Tokyo. Five thousand people lost their lives in this terrible tragedy. People from all over Japan rushed to Kobe to help out.

Six days later Seiji Ozawa was in front of the NHK Symphony Orchestra, standing before the audience at Suntory Hall, in Tokyo. The concert was going to be more meaningful than any other he had conducted, for two reasons. First, because so many Japanese had lost

The earthquake that struck Kobe, Japan, in January 1995 killed thousands of people and destroyed much of the city. Seiji dedicated a concert in nearby Tokyo to the earthquake victims.

their lives in the disaster, many people felt especially sad. Second, Seiji was being reunited with the orchestra that had once rejected him. Seiji felt that he had to find a way to help the people attending the concert cope with the tragedy.

Looking out at the audience, Seiji spoke in a gentle voice. "The damage caused by the earthquake far exceeds our imagination," said the conductor. "We would like to begin by dedicating this piece to the earthquake victims."

That said, Seiji did not step up onto the podium but instead conducted the piece from the stage floor. By that gesture, both the audience and the orchestra

36

knew Seiji understood and shared the sadness that they were feeling. Seiji also knew that the Japanese people had finally accepted him.

As a world-renowned conductor, Seiji does not perform only with the Boston Symphony. Every year he appears with many of the world's finest orchestras, including the Berlin Philharmonic, the Vienna Philharmonic, the New Japan Philharmonic, and the L'Orchestre National de France.

The most important ability of a conductor is to inspire his or her fellow musicians. This has been Seiji's strength. He is able to gently draw out the best performance from the musicians. A good conductor also has patience, understanding, a sense of humor, a willingness to accept suggestions, and the ability to be stern when necessary. Seiji has a lot of energy and continues to demand the best from himself as well as from other musicians. Most of all he loves what he does. This is clearly seen and heard in all his performances.

Besides performing on stage, most major orchestras also make recordings on videocassettes and compact discs. Seiji has conducted recordings with the Boston Symphony on more than 130 compact discs. Among them are Richard Strauss's "Don Quixote" and Schoenberg's Cello Concerto with cellist Yo-Yo Ma; Beethoven's Romances for Violin and Mendelssohn's Violin Concerto with violinist Isaac Stern; and Berlioz's "Les nuits d'été" and Debussy's "La damoiselle élue" with opera singer Frederica von Stade.

Seiji has also performed for television and video. His first video recording was of a 1986 performance of Richard Strauss's "Also sprach Zarathustra" and Brahms's Symphony No. 1, in Osaka, Japan. Seiji won an Emmy Award for Outstanding Individual Achievement for Cultural Programming in 1994 for the video program, "Dvořák in Prague: A Celebration." In this concert the Boston Symphony Orchestra performed with Yo-Yo Ma, Frederica von Stade, violinist Itzhak Perlman, and pianist Rudolf Firkušný. It was shown on PBS. Seiji has also won an Emmy Award for the PBS series, "Evening at Symphony."

   For other recordings Seiji has been given many prizes, including Grammy Awards, Grand Prix du Disques, and Edison Awards. During his career he has also received honorary degrees from several universities, including the University of San Francisco, the University of Massachusetts, and the New England Conservatory of Music. These special awards were given by the schools because they believe Seiji is someone who has done a lot to help others understand music better.

   Because of Seiji Ozawa's contributions to music and the performances he has donated to Tanglewood, the Berkshire Music Center opened the Seiji Ozawa Hall in July 1994. It can seat 1,180 people and is located in the Highwood section of Tanglewood in a part now known as Leonard Bernstein Campus.

   Seiji was very excited and proud when it was built. The hall has caught the eyes and ears of many people

To honor Seiji's commitment to the Tanglewood Music Festival, a new concert hall named Seiji Ozawa Hall opened in July 1994.

because it is beautiful to look at, and it projects the real sounds that the orchestra makes. Sound projection in concert halls is very important to musicians. They want the audience to be able to hear clearly the sounds that their instruments produce. Musicians also need to be able to hear one another on the stage. Their instruments should not sound muffled or tinny. The architects who worked on Seiji Ozawa Hall were aware of this and made sure the hall was built so that everyone would be happy with it. Musicians and audiences are very pleased with the results.

Chapter *Six*

OPENING DOORS AND BUILDING BRIDGES

Through his hard work, Maestro Ozawa is now a well-respected figure in the world of Western classical music. Seiji has never wavered in his determination to meet his goal.

"I realized what I was doing was strange only when I got to Europe," Seiji said when telling a reporter of his early days. Seiji had no idea that his chosen career would shock so many people. He also admits that he has had to pay a price over the years, but that it has all been worth it. He has opened doors and inspired many other Asian musicians to follow in his footsteps.

His family had been poor, but they encouraged him to follow his dream. During the war, when bombs were being dropped all around his home, Seiji did not know if he would live to see the next day. Later, when he traveled outside of Japan to pursue his career, there

Maestro Ozawa has contributed much to the understanding of classical music throughout the world.

was much uncertainty among Westerners about his ability. There were many obstacles, but he never gave up.

Even after Seiji was successful in the West, he was rejected in Japan. Now he is greatly admired there. The Japanese have come to realize that Seiji has never lost his love for his heritage and that he has continued to encourage the study of Western music in Japan. In 1992 Seiji founded the Saito Kinen Festival, in memory of his beloved teacher, Hideo Saito. The two-week festival is held in Matsumoto, Japan. It brings internationally famous musicians together with the Saito Kinen Orchestra. There Japanese and Western musicians perform opera, chamber music, and symphonies, making music a truly universal experience that everyone can share and enjoy. The Saito Kinen Orchestra is made up of students of Hideo Saito and their students. This group has toured Europe several times. They even opened a recent season at New York City's Carnegie Hall.

When he is not traveling around the world, either with the Boston Symphony Orchestra or as a guest conductor for other orchestras, Seiji spends part of the year with his family in Japan. His wife, Vera Ilya, whose father was Russian and whose mother was Japanese, once worked as a fashion model. Seiji married Vera in 1969. She lives in Tokyo with their two children, daughter Sheira and son Yukiyoshi, who are now both in their early twenties.

Because of what he saw during World War II and the way musicians in Japan felt about him when he was starting out, Seiji now tries hard to bridge the gap between East and West through his music. He often gives concerts dedicated to world peace and arranges for musicians from all over the world to perform together.

One of the ways in which Maestro Ozawa is most proud of bridging the gap is that he became a citizen of the United States in 1966. Seiji enjoys joint citizenship—he is a citizen of both Japan and the United States. Seiji says he decided to become a U.S. citizen because he considers himself an **ambassador** of the arts for both countries. Seiji claims he also wants to contribute to both countries as fully as possible.

Through his music Seiji Ozawa has bridged several gaps—generation, culture, and communication. He has inspired young musicians everywhere. They realize that he has achieved international recognition as a musician based on his talent and determination alone. Seiji's presence has also made a big difference in the world of Western music. He has helped bring a wider understanding both of Western music to Japan and of Japanese culture to the West.

Japan as a country has grown rapidly toward developing an understanding of Western musical

Seiji with Leonard Bernstein (center) and composer Aaron Copland at the celebration of Copland's 80th birthday.

Seiji has helped open doors from East to West, allowing an exchange of talent and technological advances in the world of classical music.

culture. Since the mid-1940s, the Japanese have tried to catch up with world standards of classical and popular music. Orchestras and opera groups were organized, music schools were established, and music festivals became common. While they absorbed the music of the West, the Japanese were also able to make an impact on the Western music world. One important contribution was the philosophy of Shin'ichi Suzuki, whose unique violin training methods are now used throughout the world. His way of teaching the violin has also been

44

applied to other string instruments, the flute, and the piano. Other important Japanese contributions are the manufacture of recording equipment, including audio and videocassettes and many types of recording machines. Instruments are also manufactured in Japan. Among the companies whose instruments are recognized for their quality and sold all over the world are Yamaha, Nippon Gakkai, and Kawai.

Communicating through music is Seiji's greatest joy. Both musicians and audiences alike respond to his honesty and warmth. As a young boy, Seiji had no idea when he was going to church with his mother or listening to the Boston Symphony Orchestra in Japan that he would later become a role model and an international star in the Western music world. He was simply doing what he enjoyed. Today the conductor has shown the world that there are no boundaries in the pursuit of dreams. Anyone who is willing to take the time to learn, to face the challenges, and is not afraid of hard work can succeed. Although Maestro Ozawa has paid the price, in return he has received priceless experiences to share with his audiences and the world.

Important Dates

1935   Born in Shenyang, China, on September 1.

1944   Returns to Japan with parents.

1951   Enrolls in the Toho Gakuen School of Music.

1959   Graduates from Toho School. Wins first prize at the International Competition of Orchestra Conductors, in Besançon, France.

1960   Wins the Koussevitzky Prize for outstanding student conductor at the Tanglewood Music Center.

1961   Leonard Bernstein makes him assistant conductor of the New York Philharmonic Orchestra; accompanies the orchestra on a tour of Japan.

1964   Becomes music director of Chicago Symphony's Ravinia Festival.

1965   Becomes music director of the Toronto Symphony.

1966   Receives United States citizenship, on December 9.

1969   Marries Vera Ilya.

1970   Becomes music director of the San Francisco Symphony Orchestra and artistic director of the Berkshire Music Festival.

1973   Becomes music director of the Boston Symphony Orchestra.

1994   Seiji Ozawa Hall, a 1,180-seat concert hall, is built at Tanglewood.

Glossary

ambassador A representative of a group or organization.

chamber music Music for a small number of instruments.

deport To send people back to their home country.

lute Pear-shaped musical instrument with strings.

maestro A master composer, conductor, or music teacher.

missionaries People sent to a foreign country to do religious or charitable work.

orchestra A large group of performers who play various musical instruments together.

protégé Someone who is guided in his or her career by an influential person.

radiation Harmful energy rays.

zither A triangular-shaped musical instrument with 30 to 40 strings that is played with the fingers.

Bibliography

Bamberger, Carl, ed. *The Conductor's Art*. McGraw Hill, 1965.

Jacobson, Bernard. *Conductors on Conducting*. Columbia Publishing Co., 1979.

Tan, Sheri. Interview with Press Office of the Boston Symphony Orchestra. May 1996.

47

Index

Bach, Johann Sebastian, 15
Beethoven, Ludwig van, 15, 37
Berkshire Music Center, Tanglewood, 20–23, 38
Berlin Philharmonic Orchestra, 24, 37
Bernstein, Leonard, 21, 23–24, 32, 43
Besançon, France, 5, 7, 9, 20
Bigot, Eugène, 20
Boston Conservatory of Music, 33–38
Boston Symphony Orchestra, 17, 20, 23, 31–35, 37–38, 42, 45
Brahms, Johannes, 15, 38

Carnegie Hall (New York), 42
Chicago Symphony Orchestra, 30

Debussy, Claude, 38

European classical music, 6–7, 15–19
"Evening at Symphony" (PBS Series), 38

Grammy Awards, 38
Grand Prix du Disques, 38

Henschel, George, 33
Higginson, Henry Lee, 33–34
Hiroshima, Japan, 13–15

Ilya, Vera, 42
International Competition of Orchestra Conductors, 5–10, 20

Japanese music, 16–17
Japan Philharmonic, 19

Karajan, Herbert von, 23–24, 32
Koussevitzky Prize, 23
Koussevitzky, Serge, 23, 33

L'Orchestre National de France, 37

Ma, Yo-Yo, 7, 37–38
Manchuria, China, 11
Matsumoto, Japan, 41
Mehta, Zubin, 21
Mendelssohn, Felix, 15, 37
Midori, 7
Münch, Charles, 18, 20, 32–33

New England Conservatory, 33, 38
New Japan Philharmonic, 28, 37
New York Philharmonic, 24
NHK Symphony Orchestra, 19, 26–29, 35–37

Osaka, Japan, 38
Ozawa, Seiji
　as ambassador of the arts, 42–45
　as assistant conductor, 24–25
　and Boston Symphony, 33–45
　citizenship, 42–43
　conducting studies, 22–25
　contribution to Asian musicians, 40–45
　cultural differences as conductor, 26–28
　early years, 11–19
　musical education, 15–19
　orchestra positions, 30–33
　piano studies, 15
　and recordings, 37–38
　Seiji Ozawa Hall (at Tanglewood), 38–39
　at Tanglewood, 20–23
　and World War II, 11–15
Ozawa, Sheira, 42
Ozawa, Yukiyoshi, 42

PBS network, 34, 38
Perlman, Itzhak, 38

Ravinia Festival, 30

Saito, Hideo, 19, 41–42
Saito Kinen Orchestra, 41–42
San Francisco Symphony Orchestra, 26–27, 30
Schoenberg, Arnold, 37
Shenyang, China, 11
Strauss, Richard, 37, 38
Suntory Hall (Tokyo), 26, 29, 35
Suzuki, Shin'ichi, 44–45

Tanglewood Music Festival, 22, 31, 39
Toho Gakuen School of Music (Tokyo), 18–19
Toronto Symphony Orchestra, 30